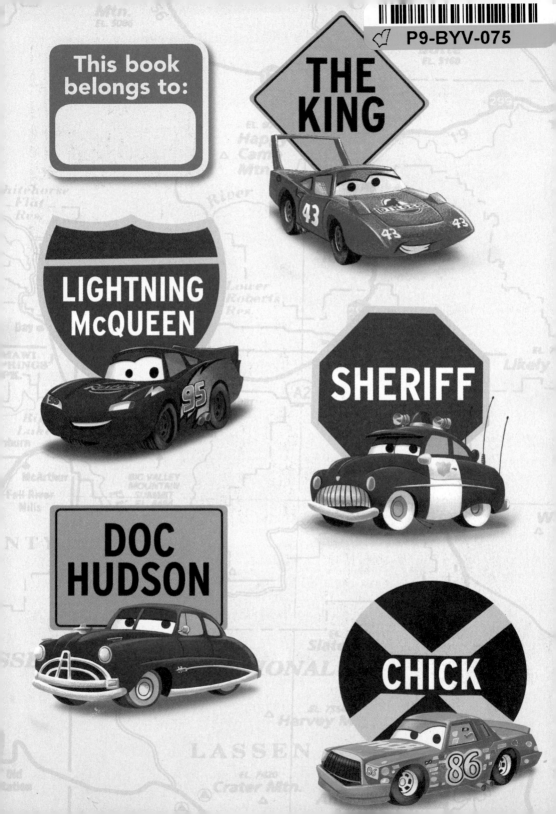

This book belongs to:

THE KING

LIGHTNING McQUEEN

SHERIFF

DOC HUDSON

CHICK

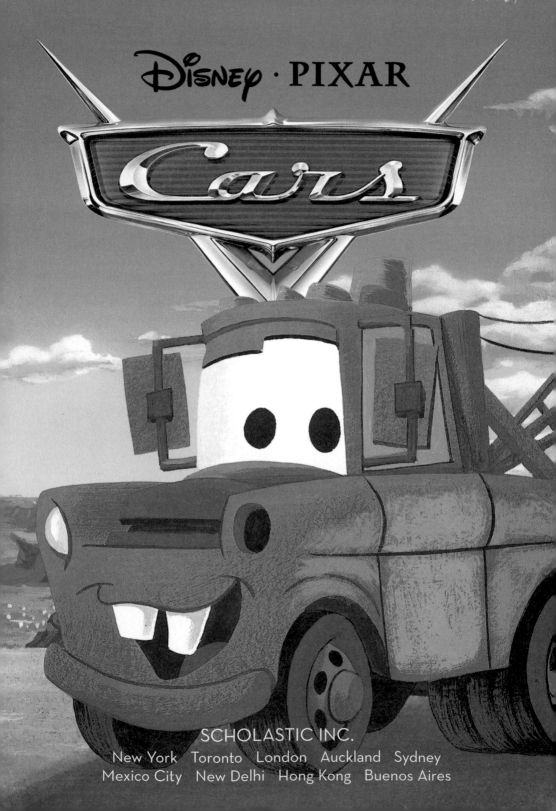

DISNEY · PIXAR

Cars

SCHOLASTIC INC.
New York Toronto London Auckland Sydney
Mexico City New Delhi Hong Kong Buenos Aires

Welcome to the biggest race of the year! To the hotshot rookie racer Lightning McQueen, it was everything he had ever worked for. Once McQueen won the Piston Cup, he would get all the fame and fortune he had always dreamed of. To McQueen, this race was *all* about winning.

It would not be an easy victory for McQueen. The King, the current champion, was doing his best to win. And the rough racer Chick was doing his worst! Chick hated coming in second place, and he wouldn't stop at dirty tricks to beat McQueen.

But McQueen had a daring plan. As everyone else pulled into pit row for a change of tires, McQueen pushed on! It was a risky move—too risky. **BLAM! BLAM!** As he was heading for victory, his two rear tires blew.

The King and Chick caught right up with McQueen!

What a race!

"That was quite a risky move, not taking tires," a reporter said to McQueen. "Are you sorry you don't have a crew chief?"

"No," McQueen said cockily, "'cause I'm a one-man show!"

The King offered the rookie some advice. "You ain't gonna win unless you got good folks behind you," The King said. "Racing ain't a one man deal."

Then the announcers reported the results. It was a three-way tie! Now the race had to be settled at a rematch in California.

McQueen was very disappointed. If his tires hadn't blown, he would probably have won. McQueen boarded Mack's trailer and they took off. Wanting to be the first one to arrive in California so he could practice, McQueen said, "We're driving straight through all night!"

He lost control of his wheels and got tangled in a fence. With the town's sheriff hot on his tail, McQueen caught hold of a statue and tore up the road. Oh boy! McQueen was in a lot of trouble now.

"Morning, sleepin' beauty!" yelled a happy tow truck, when McQueen awoke the next morning.

"What's going on here?" McQueen gasped, as he finally realized that he was trapped in the town's impound lot.

Mater, the tow truck, smiled back at him from outside the fence. "You're funny, I like you already," Mater said. "You're in Radiator Springs, the cutest little town in Carburetor County!"

McQueen looked through the fence. It didn't look so cute to him. All he saw were a few empty, broken-down buildings

McQueen was towed to the courthouse, where he faced an angry crowd. McQueen was certain they would let him go, once they realized he was a famous race car. How wrong McQueen was!

Doc Hudson, the town doctor and judge, wanted McQueen out of town. But Sally, the town attorney, convinced Doc that McQueen should stay and fix the road.

"You're going to fix the road under my supervision!" ruled Doc.

"You gotta be kidding me!" McQueen said.

McQueen protested, but there was no way out.

"This here is Bessie—finest road-pavin' machine ever built," said Doc proudly. He pointed to an enormous piece of machinery. "Hook him up, Mater!"

There was plenty of work for McQueen to do. He would have to hurry, if he was going to make it to California in time for the big race. And the race was the most important thing in McQueen's life right now.

At first, McQueen
didn't care whether he
did a good job or not. He
just had to finish so he
could leave town. In one
hour, he was done.

"It looks awful!" said Sally.

"Now it matches the rest of the town,"
McQueen replied, trying to be funny.

"The deal was you fix the road, not make it worse," grumbled Doc, when he saw the results of McQueen's efforts. "Start over again!"

"I'm not a bulldozer, I'm a race car," said McQueen.

Doc stared right at McQueen and offered him a challenge: "Then why don't we have a little race—me and you."

"If you win, you go. If I win, you do the road *my* way," said Doc. Everyone was surprised. How was Doc ever going to win a race against McQueen?

They all went to a place just outside Radiator Springs called Willys Butte. And as soon as the race began, McQueen left Doc in a cloud of dust.

Everyone looked at Doc, who slowly pulled away from the starting line. "Come on, Mater!" he said, rolling along, "might need a little help."

And sure enough, help *was* needed. McQueen was heading for a turn when he skidded and lost control. McQueen dropped off a low cliff and landed right in a cactus patch. Ouch!

"I'm starting to think he knowed you was gonna crash," giggled Mater, as he pulled McQueen back up.

It wasn't so much that McQueen had to go back, scrape off all the asphalt, and start again. What really bothered McQueen was that he had lost the race. "You drive like you fix roads," Doc said. "Lousy!"

McQueen was
a proud race car,
and he didn't
want to be called
lousy by anyone.
"I'll show him. I *will*
show him," he thought to himself. And then McQueen
went to work on the road—much more determined
than before.

The next morning, the town awoke to a newly paved section of road. It was beautiful!

"Wow," said Sally.

Even Doc looked impressed, but he still didn't trust McQueen. "He ain't finished yet," Doc said. "Now, where the heck is he?"

McQueen was out at Willys Butte! He wanted to learn to make the turn he had missed.

Doc couldn't help smiling as McQueen stumbled on the turn again and again. After a while, Doc offered McQueen some advice: turn right to go left. When Doc wasn't looking, McQueen tried it—and he missed the turn again!

Meanwhile, inspired by the new road,
all the cars in the town began fixing their
shops, making them prettier than ever.

Sally saw the
effect McQueen's
hard work was having
on the town and wanted to
thank him. So she invited him
to stay at her motel, so he
wouldn't have to sleep at the
dirty impound anymore.

"Hey, I know somethin' we can do," Mater said that night. McQueen had no idea what the silly tow truck was up to but it would probably be fun.

Soon they were sneaking into a field of sleeping tractors just outside of Radiator Springs. Yup! They were going tractor tipping!

"Just don't let Frank catch you!" warned Mater.

"Who's Frank?" asked McQueen, but Mater had already honked his horn. A sleeping tractor tipped over with a snort. McQueen, who didn't have a horn, revved his engine. Dozens of tractors tipped! Mater and McQueen laughed and laughed—until a huge harvester appeared and charged them!

"That's Frank!" screamed Mater.

The next morning, McQueen peeked into Doc's back garage. To McQueen's surprise, he found three Piston Cups hidden in all of the clutter. Doc used to be a famous race car!

At that moment,
Doc arrived. Furious
that McQueen had
discovered his secret,
Doc shooed the rookie
away, slamming the door
in McQueen's face.

McQueen was very confused. Why would a famous race car stop racing and settle down in a sleepy town?

Later that day, McQueen found Doc racing out at Willys Butte. Doc was amazing! But when he saw McQueen, Doc turned around and headed home.

"How could a car like you quit at the top of your game?" McQueen asked, after following Doc back to his garage.

"I didn't quit. They quit on ME!" Doc said bitterly. He had been damaged in a big wreck; and when he returned, a talented rookie—just like McQueen—had taken Doc's place. After that, Doc didn't trust race cars.

"Just finish that road and get outta here," Doc said.

McQueen worked all night to finish the road. Soon the little town looked shiny and new, with neon signs lighting the main street. The cars were very proud.

But, just as all the cars began cruising up and down main street, they were interrupted. A helicopter and a flood of journalists arrived. They had been searching high and low for McQueen—and now they had found him!

Mack was also there. "I'm so sorry I lost you, boss!" he said. McQueen didn't know how to say good-bye to his new friends. Sadly, he slipped into his trailer and headed off to the big race. The reporters left. And the townsfolk turned off the neon signs. Just as quickly as he had arrived, McQueen was gone again.

Finally it was race day! The King, Chick, and McQueen were waiting at the starting line, ready for the final race for this year's Piston Cup series.

But McQueen had a hard time keeping his mind on the track. He missed his friends in Radiator Springs.

McQueen was close to giving up, when suddenly a voice called out on his radio: "I didn't come all this way to see you quit!" It was Doc! "I knew you needed a Crew Chief, but I didn't know it was this bad."

What!? Doc had pulled a crew together from Radiator Springs— and now they were going to help McQueen win the race.

McQueen drove his best ever; but just as he passed Chick, the bully bumped into McQueen's back and sent him spinning towards the infield. McQueen recovered using the advice Doc had given him back at the dirt track: turn right to go left. McQueen shot back onto the track—and into the lead!

Chick was furious. "I'm not coming in last," he yelled, and rammed straight into The King! The old champion crashed.

McQueen was shocked. It reminded him of Doc. This was no way for The King to end his glorious career.

Inches before the finish line, McQueen slammed on his brakes, turned around, and went back to help The King finish his final race.

"Yeah! Whoo-hoo I won!" hollered Chick, but no one noticed him. Everyone was busy cheering McQueen and The King. McQueen had given up winning the race, proving he was a true champion. Doc couldn't have been prouder.

McQueen set up his new racing headquarters at Radiator Springs. Doc was his new crew chief and occasional racing partner. It seemed the hotshot rookie still had a lot to learn from the old timer. McQueen felt so good to be among his friends again.

THE END

EYE SPY
Race back into the book and find these pictures.